STEAM GUIDES IN

A P P

DEVELOPMENT

Ruth M. Kirk

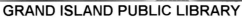

ROURKE
Educational Media
rourkeeducationalmedia.com

Scan for Related Titles and
Teacher Resources.

Before Reading:

Building Academic Vocabulary and Background Knowledge

Before reading a book, it is important to tap into what your child or students already know about the topic. This will help them develop their vocabulary, increase their reading comprehension, and make connections across the curriculum.

1. *Look at the cover of the book. What will this book be about?*
2. *What do you already know about the topic?*
3. *Let's study the Table of Contents. What will you learn about in the book's chapters?*
4. *What would you like to learn about this topic? Do you think you might learn about it from this book? Why or why not?*
5. *Use a reading journal to write about your knowledge of this topic. Record what you already know about the topic and what you hope to learn about the topic.*
6. *Read the book.*
7. *In your reading journal, record what you learned about the topic and your response to the book.*
8. *After reading the book complete the activities below.*

Content Area Vocabulary
Read the list. What do these words mean?

calling
device
download
facilitate
feasible
function
grid
legendary
minimize
potential
profit
proportions
punch line
setup
subtle

After Reading:

Comprehension and Extension Activity

After reading the book, work on the following questions with your child or students in order to check their level of reading comprehension and content mastery.

1. *What are bits made up of?* (Summarize)
2. *How do artists submit their work to a programmer?* (Infer)
3. *Can you make an app without knowing a coding language?* (Asking questions)
4. *Why won't your touch screen work if you are wearing gloves?* (Text to self connection)
5. *In what year was the iPhone introduced?* (Asking questions)

Extension Activity

It's hard to imagine that there was once no such thing as apps for your smartphone or tablet. Using a piece of poster board, make a timeline with all the apps you have on your phone. Do some research on the Internet and list the information you find about those apps, such as who created them, when they were created, what they do, etc. Also research other apps that could be helpful to you for school or homework.

Table of Contents

A Brief History of Apps: Forward Fast

Are you looking for the best ice cream shop? Eager to see how your friend's haircut turned out? Hoping there's a game to help you study for that test tomorrow? You probably turn to an app in all those situations and many more. Let's explore how the world of apps is connected with the world of STEAM. Without science, technology, engineering, art, and math, no one would ever have even seen an app!

Technology today provides an app for just about anything you can think of.

And just what is an app? Less than forty years ago, only computer programmers used that word. It was a shorter way to refer to computer applications or software. Back then, almost all telephones were connected with wires, and you had to be at your office or home to make or answer a call. Just a small percentage of offices and almost no homes had computers.

Then new technologies began to transform our daily lives. Cellular phones were invented that could be carried with you everywhere you went. Computers became smaller and cheaper every year, and eventually became a part of nearly every business and household. The Internet evolved into a system linking almost all the computers around the globe.

Banking and medical services available through cell phones and the Internet have improved the lives of people in developing countries.

Steve Jobs
1955 - 2011

Hundreds of customers waited in line outside Apple stores to buy the first iPhones in June 2007.

In 2007, Steve Jobs, the head of Apple, Inc., made a presentation that has now become **legendary**. Pacing on the stage, he announced that Apple was introducing three products that would change everything: a music player with touch controls, a revolutionary mobile phone, and an Internet communication **device**. Then he delivered the **punch line**: "These are not three separate devices. This is one device, and we are calling it iPhone."

The iPhone came with apps like email, an Internet browser, and maps already installed. Soon, users of the phone were able to **download** additional apps from an online store. Other brands and types of smartphones now compete with the iPhone, and people all over the world increasingly rely on smartphones in their daily lives.

STEAM
Fast Fact!

Apple awarded prizes to the users who downloaded milestone apps from its App Store. A woman in England downloaded "Paper Glider" as the 10-billionth app; a man in China downloaded "Where's My Water," a physics-based puzzler as the 25-billionth app; and a man from Ohio downloaded a word game, "Say the Same Thing," as the 50-billionth app.

Total App Downloads from Apple's App Store

	July 2008	April 2009	January 2011	March 2012	May 2013	June 2015
billion						
■illion						
■illion						
■illion						
■lion						
■nch						

Worldwide iPhone availability

iPhone availability since the release of iPhone 3G

Having a touch screen and the ability to download apps from an online store are the two features that now qualify a phone as a smartphone. People can download those same apps onto their larger devices known as tablets.

Smartphones and tablets together make up the category of mobile devices. When people talk about apps, they usually mean native mobile apps, or apps designed specifically to run on mobile devices, rather than on desktop or laptop computers.

Let's take a closer look at those features that mobile devices have in common: touch screen and download capability.

Touch Screens and Downloads: Magic on the Screen

You touch the screen of your phone and nothing happens. Why won't that app open? Are you wearing gloves? Take them off and try again, and the screen works fine. Why the difference?

Most touch screens today are called capacitive, meaning they work when they are touched by something that can conduct electricity. The skin of your finger has that ability, but an ordinary glove does not. You'll need special gloves with metal woven in to both stay warm and use your touch screen.

If you could take your screen apart, you would see that it is made up of layers. The top layer is an extra strong type of glass. Underneath is a **grid** made of wires, each one smaller than a human hair. The grid has an electric charge running through it at a certain voltage, or strength.

A stylus for a capacitive screen must contain material that conducts electricity.

When you touch the screen, some of the charge goes to your finger, lowering the voltage at that spot. The computer in your device knows where you touched the screen, whether you touched in one place or two places, or whether your finger moved across the screen. With that information, it's able to carry out the **function** you want.

Maybe you touched the icon of an online store in order to download an app. A lot of activity goes on behind the scenes to allow an app to travel over the Internet and install itself on your device.

cell tower

Cell towers provide a way for information to travel over the Internet.

Pictures, words, sounds, and all the other information that gets sent to you over the Internet must be translated into the form of binary information, or bits, to make the journey. Bits are made up of ones and zeros.

Quantities of Binary Information

Byte	8 bits	1 keyboard character
Kilobyte	about 1,000 bytes	5-page paper
Megabyte	about 1,000 kilobytes	42 seconds of MP3
Gigabyte	about 1,000 megabytes	about 2 hours of video

Bits can travel three ways: as radio waves through the air, as electric pulses through copper wires, or as light beams through fiber optic cables.

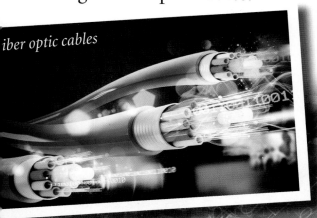

iber optic cables

Entrepreneurs have proposed placing thousands of satellites in low Earth orbit to provide Internet service.

Your order for an app may first travel through the air as radio waves from your device to reach a machine in your home called a router/modem. From there, the bits travel through a wire, probably a copper one, as electric pulses. If bits need to travel between continents, they flow as light waves through fiber optic cables on the ocean floor.

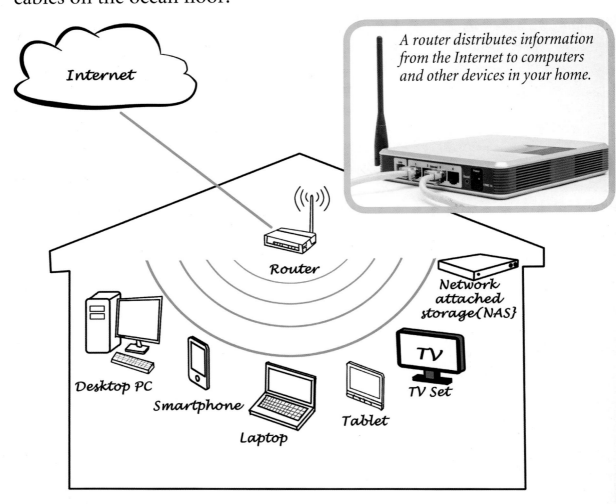

A router distributes information from the Internet to computers and other devices in your home.

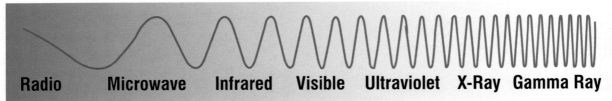

Light waves are measured in wavelengths, which is the distance between the high point of a wave and the low point of the wave beside it.

Sooner than it might seem possible, the bits of information you requested reach your device, and voila! An icon for the new app appears on your screen, like magic, just waiting for your touch!

STEAM
Fast Fact!

Shark attack! Look out Internet cable! Sharks sometimes try to sink their big pointy teeth into the fiber optic cables on the ocean floor. Google shields its cables with a strong fabric, similar to what is used in bulletproof vests.

Artists at Work: Pleasing the Eye

Why does each of the icons on your device have its own distinctive look? Graphic artists were at work! Can you close your eyes and picture the icons for the apps you use most? If you look at a screen full of icons, are some easier than others to find at a glance?

Facebook is the most used app in the world.

An effective icon will help to determine the app's virality, one of the two factors that work together to determine whether it will be useful or produce a **profit**. Virality is a measure of how many different people download the app. The other factor is engagement, or how many people will use the app repeatedly. Whether the screens of the app have an appealing look affects its engagement.

Graphic artists are faced with many decisions for every app project they tackle. The work of an artist is of great importance in gaming apps, and an artist chooses the colors and layout even in apps that are mostly text. Well-designed apps make it easy for users to navigate within the app, and easy to understand the content being communicated.

STEAM
Fast Fact!

Many artists whose work appears on apps use a graphics tablet that is connected to their computer screen. These tablets are more precise and sensitive to touch than a typical touch screen. An artist can choose to create an image on a tablet with an array of tools, including pen-like styluses and even brushes.

Designers at Apple have posted advice about designing apps for different purposes. For an app meant to help someone accomplish a serious task, they suggest **subtle** decorative features that don't require too much of the user's attention. But for a gaming app, they recommend an exciting appearance that will encourage discovery.

The design of an icon must work when it is surrounded by other icons as well as when it is set apart.

Artists submit their work to a programmer in the form of an electronic file. If the art is a photograph, it would be submitted as a file type known as a raster file, meaning the image is made up of a group of pixels or dots of color arranged in a rectangular grid. A different type of file used for art is called a vector file. In a vector file, an image is composed of anchor points that are connected by lines called paths. Computer software uses mathematical equations to create the paths, and to keep the **proportions** of the image the same if it needs to be enlarged or reduced.

96 ppi

192 ppi

384 ppi

A display that you hold close to your eyes, like a cell phone, needs to have a greater pixels per inch ratio than one you view from a distance, like a television.

STEAM
Fast Fact!

When you're dealing with cameras, images, or displays, pixel density mostly determines how sharp they are. Pixels are the tiny dots that make up an image or display, and the smaller they are, the clearer the image will look. Whether measured by pixels per inch, ppi or by dots per inch, dpi, more is better.

To better appreciate what a graphic artist does, try to recreate the home screens of a few apps using a pencil and paper. You just might find that graphic art is your **calling**!

Coding: Everyone's Invited

What language or languages do you speak? English, Spanish, Mandarin? Do computers speak those languages? Not exactly. So, if you want to make an app, how are you going to make your computer understand you?

At the most basic level, computers only understand machine language, and it's binary, made up of a string of zeros and ones. To translate machine language into something easier to use, engineers invented programming or coding languages like Java and Python. Learning to code means learning to use those languages, and it takes some time and effort.

```css
----- Masthead ---------- */

ar { display: none; border-bottom:1px solid #cecece; padding: 10px 0; }
{ text-indent: -9999px; display: inline-block; background: url(../images/logo.png) no-repeat
n { color:#fff; background: #333 }


----- Masthead ---------- */

----- Content ---------- */
-------- Text styles -------- */

icle { font-family: @fontFace; font-size:13px; color:#454545; line-height: normal;
1, h2, h3, h4, h5, h6 { font-family: @fontFace; line-height: 1; margin-bottom: 10px; color:#
1.unline, h2.unline, h3.unline, h4.unline, h5.unline, h6.unline { border-bottom: 1px solid #
1 { font-size: 24px; margin-bottom:15px;}
2 { font-size: 20px; margin-bottom:13px;}
3 { font-size: 16px; margin-bottom:10px;}
h4 { font-size: 15px; margin-bottom:5px;}
h5 { font-size: 14px; margin-bottom:4px;}
h6 { font-size: 13px; margin-bottom:3px;}
strong {font-weight: bold; }
ul,ol { list-style:none;
  margin: 0 0 15px 0;
  padding: 0 0 0 20px;
  li {list-style-type: disc; color:#4d4c4c
    a{ color:#4d4c4c;
      &:hover { text-decoration:none; col
    }
    ul.ol {margin: 0 0 5px 0;
```

```javascript
$("#fin").slid

});
function p(a) {
    a = a.replace(//(\
    gm, q(a);
    = q(a);
    replace(//
```

You can make an app without knowing a coding language. Engineers at the Massachusetts Institute of Technology (MIT) and Google worked together to create the free program App Inventor. You've probably heard the phrase "the tip of the iceberg." That could describe your part if you make an app with App Inventor.

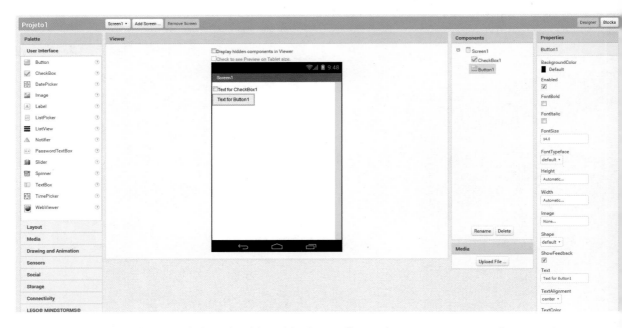

App Inventor uses drag-and-drop building blocks to allow a beginner to succeed in creating an app.

Since other people have done the coding to make your part easy, is there any reason for you to learn to code? Leaders in the field of technology can give you plenty of reasons. They say learning to code makes you like a wizard with superpowers. They believe that studying computer science teaches students to use computational thinking.

People, not computers, do computational thinking. It involves understanding a problem well enough to know how a computer might be useful in finding a solution. One aspect of computational thinking is decomposing a problem, or breaking it down into manageable chunks. For example, if you're studying for a test with two friends, you might each teach the others one third of the material.

Another element of computational thinking is using abstraction, or separating out details that are not needed in a given situation. You use abstraction when you make maps because maps don't show all the details of a place. They just show important places or routes.

Using algorithms is also a part of computational thinking. An algorithm is a sequence of steps to follow to complete a task. An effective algorithm helps to **minimize** the steps in a process. Suppose you need to determine a secret number between 1 and 100 by only asking yes and no questions. Asking if the number is larger than 50 would be a better first step than asking if the number is larger than 98.

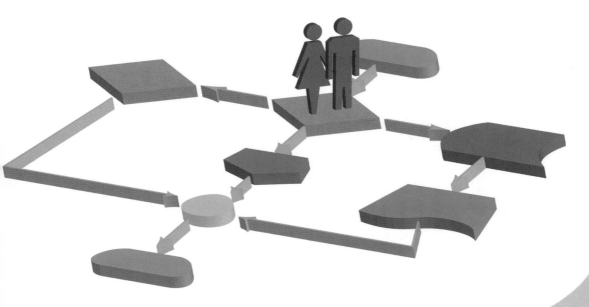

A flow chart communicates the steps of an algorithm.

Giving every student in every school the opportunity to learn computer science is the goal of an organization called Code.org. Check out the website to get inspired and get started!

STEAM
Fast Fact !

Hour of Code is a global movement organized by Code.org to show that anybody can learn the basics of coding. Most Hour of Code events take place in December during Computer Science Education Week, but events can take place any time of the year.

Hour of Code Statistics

Number of participants	**210,601,670**
Lines of code written	**11,151,730,618**
Countries represented	**180+**
Languages in which tutorial is available	**40**

When you think about an app development company, what do you picture? You might imagine a big open room with an artist drawing on an electronics tablet, while someone across the way is writing the text, and a programmer in the corner is busy writing code.

A **setup** of that type is possible, but often, the people who work on apps are sitting not across the room, but across the world from each other. The artist might be in Romania, the programmer in Singapore, and the writer in the United States. Video chat apps and email **facilitate** this arrangement. But there is a catch. Sometimes workers live in different time zones, so the sleeping time may happen while their colleagues in another country are working.

STEAM
Fast Fact !

People working on the same app, but who are physically far away from each other use video chat apps, just as you may. Did you realize that your phone or tablet has two cameras, one main camera and one back camera? It's the back camera, the lower quality one, that video chat apps mainly use.

Why isn't it the same time for people all over the Earth? Let's start with this idea: people want noon to mean the middle of the day wherever they are. Since the Earth is a sphere, rotating on its axis as it revolves around the sun, when it's light on one side, it's dark on the other.

WORLD STANDARD TIME ZONES

-11	-10	-9	-8	-7	-6	-5	-4	-3	-2	-1	0	+1	+2	+3	+4	+5

ARCTIC OCEAN

Baffin Bay

Davis Strait

Hudson Bay

Labrador Sea

Gulf of Alaska

NORTH PACIFIC OCEAN

NORTH ATLANTIC OCEAN

Caribbean Sea

Gulf of Mexico

+13   -9½

SOUTH PACIFIC OCEAN

SOUTH ATLANTIC OCEAN

-5

-3

-3

SOUTHERN OCEAN

ALASKA (UNITED STATES)

CANADA

UNITED STATES

MEXICO

PERU   BRAZIL

BOLIVIA

ARGENTINA

Falkland Islands (U.K.)

St. Georgia and South Sandwich Islands

1:00	2:00	3:00	4:00	5:00	6:00	7:00	8:00	9:00	10:00	11:00	12:00	13:00	14:00	15:00	16:00	17
-11	-10	-9	-8	-7	-6	-5	-4	-3	-2	-1	0	+1	+2	+3	+4	+5

Over 100 years ago, an international group decided to divide the Earth into 24 time zones, corresponding to the 24 hours of the day. By dividing the 360 degrees that make up the Earth's sphere by the 24 hours in a day, you come out with time zones that are each 15 degrees wide. Going east, the time gets later by one hour every time you enter a new time zone.

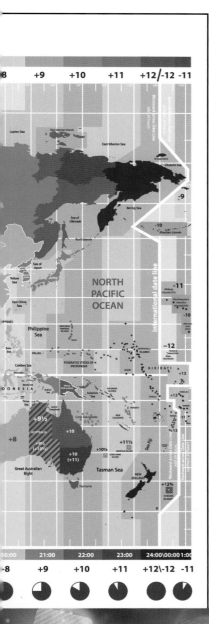

New York	Bucharest	Singapore
12 MIDNIGHT	7:00 AM	1:00 PM
1:00 AM	8:00 AM	2:00 PM
2:00 AM	9:00 AM	3:00 PM
3:00 AM	10:00 AM	4:00 PM
4:00 AM	11:00 AM	5:00 PM
5:00 AM	12 NOON	6:00 PM
6:00 AM	1:00 PM	7:00 PM
7:00 AM	2:00 PM	8:00 PM
8:00 AM	3:00 PM	9:00 PM
9:00 AM	4:00 PM	10:00 PM
10:00 AM	5:00 PM	11:00 PM
11:00 AM	6:00 PM	12 MIDNIGHT
12 NOON	7:00 PM	1:00 AM
1:00 PM	8:00 PM	2:00 AM
2:00 PM	9:00 PM	3:00 AM
3:00 PM	10:00 PM	4:00 AM
4:00 PM	11:00 PM	5:00 AM
5:00 PM	12 MIDNIGHT	6:00 PM
6:00 PM	1:00 AM	7:00 PM
7:00 PM	2:00 AM	8:00 PM
8:00 PM	3:00 AM	9:00 PM
9:00 PM	4:00 AM	10:00 PM
10:00 PM	5:00 AM	11:00 PM
11:00 PM	6:00 AM	12 NOON

The imaginary north-south line (shown at zero on the map) that runs through Greenwich, England, is the basis for the world's time zone system.

Working with people in different time zones can have both advantages and disadvantages. Suppose app designers in America need to have programming work completed before they can continue their design work. It works well if the programming can be done in India, where the workday is going on while the American designers are sleeping. A disadvantage is the difficulty of discussing ongoing work.

Do you have friends or relatives who live in different time zones? What is your strategy for communicating with them?

PACIFIC
OCEAN

RALIA

NEW ZEALAND

STEAM
Fast Fact!

China and India are among a small group
of countries that don't follow the worldwide
time zone system exactly. All clocks in China
are set to the time of the capital city, Beijing.
In India, the time is the same all over the
country and their time is out of synch with
the system by 30 minutes.

The Engineering Process: Finding a Solution

Let's imagine that your big brother has taken up jogging. The good news is that his fitness is improving. The bad news is that he sometimes brushes up against some poison ivy. Itch, itch, itch! Could you design an app to help?

Experienced app designers would advise you to follow the engineering process. How does that process differ from the scientific method you've used to complete your science fair project? Well, scientists start with a question and move towards one correct answer. Engineers start with a human problem and seek to find a solution to that problem through a design. Often, more than one solution is **feasible**.

STEAM Fast Fact!

If the engineering process appeals to you, investigate the eighteen types of engineering described on the website of the National Action Council for Minorities in Engineering. The Council's members hold the belief that diversity drives innovation. Do you agree?

The first step is to define the problem. Warning: Skipping this step may be hazardous to your app! Jumping right into action on a project can be tempting. But no one wants to put a lot of time, energy, and money into solving a problem that doesn't exist.

You've heard of putting yourself in someone else's shoes? In this case, you'll need to imagine yourself in the running shoes of your app's **potential** users.

Will they use their phones to stop and identify the evil plant while they're on the trail? Or should your app help them memorize the look of the plant ahead of time?

You also need to think about criteria and constraints, two words that are as familiar to engineers as salt and pepper. The criteria are the characteristics of a successful solution, like having **accurate** content. Constraints are limits, like on the amount of time allowed to complete the project.

Research and brainstorming are important, too. Does the appearance of poison ivy change with the seasons? Would drawings or photographs work best? What other apps are effective in helping people remember information? Next might come sketching all the screens of the app on paper and figuring out how they would connect.

Finally, you're ready to sit down at your computer to make a prototype, or example. Then you could ask some people to test it, and get as much feedback as you can.

STEAM Fast Fact!

Google gets feedback on the Google app by inviting the public to test the new versions of it. This type of testing by the intended audience is the second phase of testing, or beta testing. The first phase, or alpha testing, is done within the company.

Based on the test results, you'll probably want to return to an earlier step to make improvements. Then you'll be ready to test again. Repeating steps to get better and better results is known as iteration.

1. Define the problem.

2. Research and brainstorm—define how your app would work the best.

3. Sketch all of the app screens on paper.

Ways to Get in the Field

If you'd like to know more about app development, here are some suggestions:

- Join an after-school coding or app development club.
- Analyze several similar apps to see what makes one better than another.
- Create an app to solve a problem at your school using the App Inventor website.
- Try out coding using the tutorials at www.code.org.
- Follow a blog about a type of app that interests you.

4. Make a prototype.

5. Ask people to test it and get feedback.

Glossary

calling (KAWL-ing): your calling is the job, profession, or other important thing that you want to do in your life

device (di-VISE): a piece of equipment that does a particular job

download (DOUN-lohd): to transfer information from a larger to a smaller computer, or from an Internet location to your own computer

facilitate (fuh-SIL-i-tate): to make something easier

feasible (FEE-zuh-buhl): able to be achieved successfully

function (FUHNGK-shuhn): one of the things that a computer program can do

grid (grid): a network of uniformly spaced vertical and horizontal lines that forms a regular pattern of squares

legendary (LEJ-uhn-der-ee): very well known, usually because of some remarkable event or action

minimize (MIN-uh-mize): to reduce something as much as possible

potential (puh-TEN-shuhl): possible, but not yet actual or real

profit (PRAH-fit): the amount of money left after all the costs of running a business have been subtracted from the money earned

proportions (pruh-POR-shuhnz): the measurements or size of something

punch line (puhnch line): the last line of a joke or story that makes it funny or surprising

setup (SET-uhp): the way that something is arranged

subtle (SUHT-uhl): clever and not overly obvious

Index

Show What You Know

1. What was surprising about the presentation in 2007 by Steve Jobs?
2. Why does a touch screen respond to your finger?
3. How does graphic design relate to the purpose of an app?
4. Why is learning to code beneficial?
5. How do the scientific method and the engineering process differ from each other?

Websites To Visit

www.appinventor.mit.edu

www.code.org

www.computerhistory.org

About The Author

Ruth M. Kirk writes nonfiction for young readers from her home in North Carolina, and also teaches English as a Second Language. She enjoys discovering new information by using and sharing apps with her family and friends.

Meet The Author!
www.meetREMauthors.com

PHOTO CREDITS: Cover: sketches © Natykach Nataliia, tablet with floating apps © ra2studio; Pages 4-5 phone showing google © maxpro, phone with snapchat © essay, woman © file404, globe © stockmdm; pages 6-7 Steve Jobs © mylerdude, i-phone 1G © cristographic, map © Lokal_Profil, Eraserhead1, hand with phone © Alexey Boldin; pages 8-9 finger on App store © ymgerman, tablet and phone © Pieter Beens, using tablet © Bloomua; pages 10-11 touching phone © BsWei, using stylus © into, illustration phone © Vector pro; pages 12-13 www.BillionPhotos.com, inset photo © Peezaar; pages 14-15 binaryy code © wavebreakmedia, satellite © bluebay, circuit board © ricked, fiber optics © alphaspirit; pages 16-17 © electromagnetic waves Inductiveload, NASA, home network © arka38, router © JonikFoto.pl, shark © Matt9122; pages 18-19 phone with floating apps © Sergey Nivens, Facebook on phone © weedezign; pages 20-21 designers © Jacob Lund, apps © MCruzUA; pages 22-23 portrait of woman © BestPhotoStudio, designer © baranq, apps © Seamartini Graphics; pages 24-25 © hands at computer © Morrowind, close-up code © Mclek; pages 26-27 screen shot © MIT Media Lab, wizard © Tepeter; pages 28-29 students with laptop © ProStockStudio, phone © Alexey Boldin; pages 30-31 flow chart © limn, girl with thought bubble © Creativa Images; pages 32-33 © vectorfusionart, phone with Skype © I AM NIKOM; pages 34-35 Earth © Skylines, map © Jktu_21; pages 36-37 women at computer © Stuart Jenner, map © ctrlaplus; pages 38-39 guy jogging © fantom_rd, poison ivy plant © Tim Mainiero; pages 40-41 poison ivy illustration © Luciano Cosmo, girl with thought bubble © Andy Dean Photography, takeng a photo © vvoe; pages 42-43 © girl Andy Dean Photography, poison ivy close ups © Stuart Monk, on tree © Dejan Stanisavljevic, illustration of sketches © Mascha Tace, wire frames © Hardyguardy, group of people © Rawpixel.com. All images from Shutterstock.com except pages 6, 7, 26

Edited by: Keli Sipperley

Cover and Interior design by: Nicola Stratford   www.nicolastratford.com

Library of Congress PCN Data

STEAM Guides in App Development / Ruth M. Kirk
(STEAM Every Day)
ISBN 978-1-68191-709-2 (hard cover)
ISBN 978-1-68191-810-5 (soft cover)
ISBN 978-1-68191-906-5 (e-Book)

Library of Congress Control Number: 2016932587

Rourke Educational Media
Printed in the United States of America, North Mankato, Minnesota

Also Available as:

ROURKE'S e-Books